THE STORY SO FAR

ZACK HAD THOUGHT ALL THERE WAS TO FOOTBALL WAS KICKING A BALL; HE CERTAINLY HADN'T EXPECTED TO CROSS SWORDS WITH THE MAFIA. THEN AGAIN, IT WASN'T IN ALAN'S GAME PLAN TO BE THE VICTIM OF A GYPSY CURSE EITHER! THE LIFE OF A PREMIERSHIP FOOTBALLER CERTAINLY ISN'T STRAIGHT FORWARD.

THE COMETS' CLASH WITH F.C. COLISEUM IN ROME ENDED IN A DRAW; AND BACK AT HOME THEY MASSACRED THE MARAUDERS AND SMASHED WESTFIELD UNITED'S DEFENCE. THIS HAS THEM AT THE TOP OF THE LEAGUE, BUT HOW LONG CAN THEY STAY THERE?

THE BEAUTY OF ROME...

AH, THE EUROPEAN CUP!
A CHANCE FOR THE TEAM
TO ENJOY THE UNDISCOVERED
WONDERS OF OUR EUROPEAN
FRIENDS, LIKE...

AND THE NEVER ENDING RAIN OF GLASGOW...

THE BRAVEHEARTS ARE A
GOAL UP RIGHT NOW WITH
15 MINS TO GO. THE COMETS
SIMPLY HAVE TO SCORE!

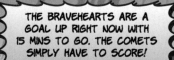

SHHLOOOOOSH!!

...AND THE CONDITIONS ON THE
PITCH ARE TREACHEROUS!
ZACK CASSIDY'S DOWN!

2

SAMPILSON!

THE SHORT PASS
WITH SAMPILSON

FORGIVE SENOR MONK, BUT IN BRAZIL WE NEVER HAVE TO FIGHT WATER LIKE ZIS. TO PASS SHORT AND ACURATELY USE ZE INSTEP OF YOUR BOOT AND HIT THROUGH. ZE MORE YOU FOLLOW THROUGH, ZE FASTER ZE BALL GO! CAREFUL THOUGH, ZIS IS EASY TO READ...

THAT WAS TERRIBLE, LUCKILY HERE'S PRESTON WITH A BELTER!

WHUMMP!

MEANWHILE, IN THE CHANGING ROOMS...

BUT, MR. CHAIRMAN, YOU'RE TALKING ABOUT THE FUTURE OF THE CLUB!

EXACTLY **HOW MUCH** DEBT ARE WE IN?

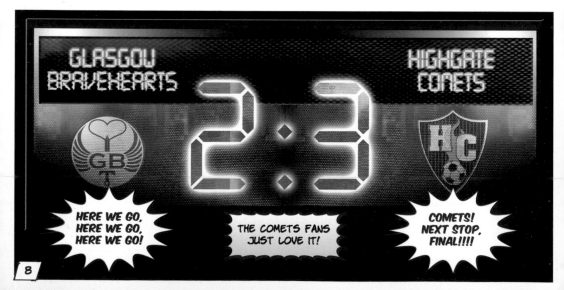

YOU HAVE TO PERSEVERE. WITH A SQUAD LIKE OURS, WE KNEW WE'D GET A BREAK IN THE END.

OR THREE!

AND WHAT ABOUT THE TITLE? IS IT A TWO HORSE RACE? YOU AND THE MERSEY FERRYMEN?

IF IT IS, THERE'S ONLY ONE HORSE THAT'S GONNA WIN IT, ISN'T THERE, LUKEY BOY...

TOO RIGHT! BRING ON THE GALACTICOS!

FUNNY LUKE SHOULD SAY THAT...

MR. PRESTON? WE'RE FROM MADRID GALACTICOS...

COULD WE HAVE A WORD..?

10

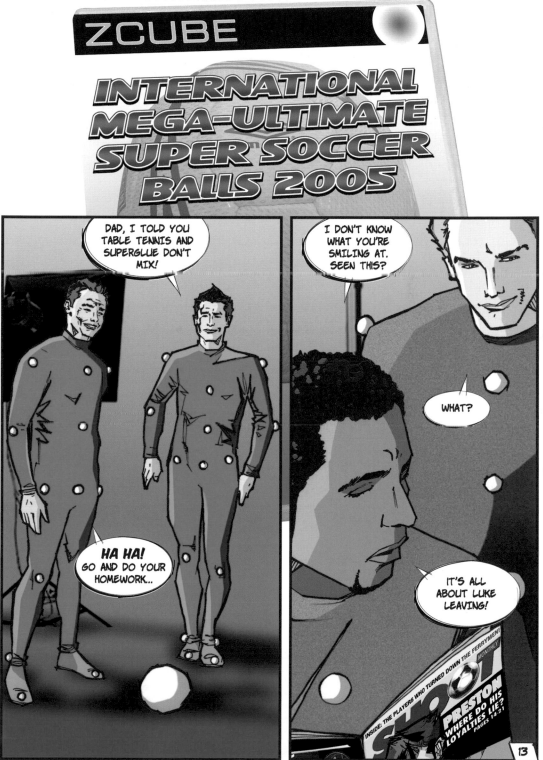

15

AGH!

35 MINUTES...

oOF!

SKRITCH!
SKRATCH!
SKRITCH!

ZACK CASSIDY GETS IN THE WAY AGAIN. TOTALLY OFF FORM!

42 MINUTES...

AT LAST! A BEAUTIFUL HEADER THERE. LOOKS LIKE ZACK MAY SAVE HIS REPUTATION YET... 1-0

HUMPH!

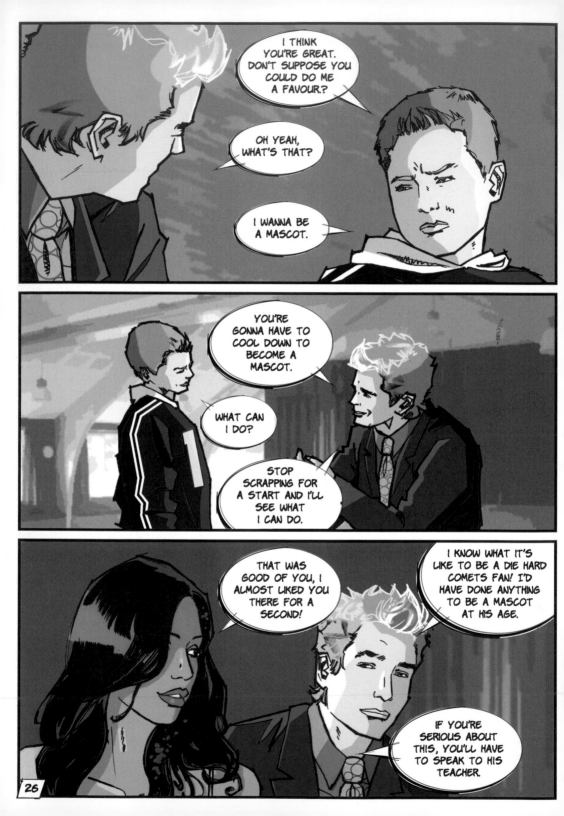

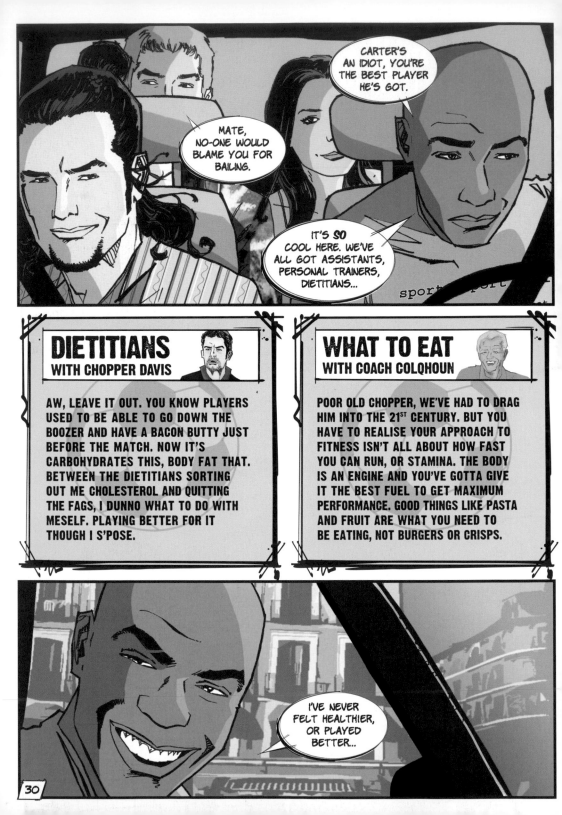

CARTER'S AN IDIOT, YOU'RE THE BEST PLAYER HE'S GOT.

MATE, NO-ONE WOULD BLAME YOU FOR BAILING.

IT'S **SO** COOL HERE. WE'VE ALL GOT ASSISTANTS, PERSONAL TRAINERS, DIETITIANS...

DIETITIANS
WITH CHOPPER DAVIS

AW, LEAVE IT OUT. YOU KNOW PLAYERS USED TO BE ABLE TO GO DOWN THE BOOZER AND HAVE A BACON BUTTY JUST BEFORE THE MATCH. NOW IT'S CARBOHYDRATES THIS, BODY FAT THAT. BETWEEN THE DIETITIANS SORTING OUT ME CHOLESTEROL AND QUITTING THE FAGS, I DUNNO WHAT TO DO WITH MESELF. PLAYING BETTER FOR IT THOUGH I S'POSE.

WHAT TO EAT
WITH COACH COLQHOUN

POOR OLD CHOPPER, WE'VE HAD TO DRAG HIM INTO THE 21ST CENTURY. BUT YOU HAVE TO REALISE YOUR APPROACH TO FITNESS ISN'T ALL ABOUT HOW FAST YOU CAN RUN, OR STAMINA. THE BODY IS AN ENGINE AND YOU'VE GOTTA GIVE IT THE BEST FUEL TO GET MAXIMUM PERFORMANCE. GOOD THINGS LIKE PASTA AND FRUIT ARE WHAT YOU NEED TO BE EATING, NOT BURGERS OR CRISPS.

I'VE NEVER FELT HEALTHIER, OR PLAYED BETTER...

GAME OF THE DAY

SPORT

OFFICIAL PREMIERSHIP TABLE

		P	W	D	L	PTS
1	HIGHGATE COMETS	29	23	4	2	72
2	MERSEY FERRYMEN	29	22	6	1	72
3	NEWCASTLE NUKES	29	21	7	1	70
4	CHELSEA BLUES	29	21	5	3	68
5	TOTTENHAM TIGERS	29	19	7	3	64
6	SOUTHAMPTON SHARKS	29	18	7	4	61
7	WESTFIELD UTD	29	18	6	5	60
8	DAGENHAM DAMAGE	29	16	10	3	58
9	ROYSTON ROVERS	29	16	9	4	57
10	CARDIFF DRAGONS	29	14	9	6	51

I APPRECIATE THE EXTRA REVENUE THAT WINNING THE TREBLE WILL GENERATE.

I'LL FIND A BUYER. I'LL DO ANYTHING IT TAKES...

THEN WE DON'T NEED TO SELL..?

IT'S NOT UP FOR DISCUSSION, MR. CARTER. IF WE DON'T MAKE A PAYMENT NOW, WE'LL BE PUT IN ADMINISTRATION.

FOR SOME PEOPLE FOOTBALL MEANS MORE THAN JUST MONEY!

I'LL GET THE MONEY IF IT KILLS ME!

45

49

WELL, NO-ONE EXPECTED THIS!!

HIGHGATE COMETS

NEWCASTLE NUKES

0:0

"IT'S ABI HERE IN THE STUDIO. DESPITE HAVING TWO OF THE HIGHEST SCORING OFFENSIVE LINE UPS IN THE LEAGUE, YOU'VE GOT TO GIVE IT TO THE DEFENCES TODAY. WE'RE STILL GOALLESS, FOLKS, BUT AS IT'S THE CUP SEMI-FINAL REPLAY WE'RE GETTING A RESULT TODAY ONE WAY OR ANOTHER. WHAT DO YOU THINK, LAWRIE?"

"CUP TIES AT THIS STAGE USUALLY GO ONE WAY OR ANOTHER — EITHER REALLY TIGHT DEFENSIVE PLAY OR ALL OUT WAR!!"

"AND DON'T FORGET IT'S EXTRA TOUGH FOR THE COMETS. CARTER'S TRYING TO HOLD OFF HIS CREDITORS, MAYBE EVEN ATTRACT A BUYER. THIS REALLY IS MAKE OR BREAK FOR THEM, THEY'VE GOT TO WIN! IF THEY LOSE THIS HE'LL HAVE TO SELL. I WONDER WHAT MUST BE GOING THROUGH HIS MIND AT THE MOMENT."

"I DON'T KNOW, ABI, THE PRESSURE MUST BE ENORMOUS. BUT ONE THING'S FOR CERTAIN — HE'S NOT GONNA WANT IT TO GET TO PENALTIES..."

110 MINUTES...

120 MINUTES...

AND THEY JUST CAN'T SEEM TO SHAKE THE MIGHTY NUKES. THE COMETS ARE STARTING TO LOOK TIRED.

CARTER'S MAKING SOME LAST-MINUTE CHANGES.

DEFENDER GOMO IS OFF FOR DI FLORES AND MIDFIELDER SAMPILSON FOR THE FRENCHMAN, JUILLET.

WHEEEEEEP!

OH DEAR, PENALTIES...

WES VS WESSON...

RAFÉ VS TWINRIVERS...

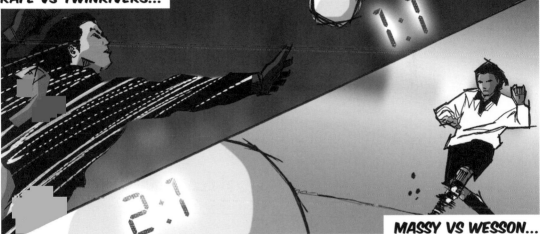

MASSY VS WESSON...

BENETEZ VS TWINRIVERS...

PRESTON VS WESSON...

SCHOX VS TWINRIVERS...

OFFERS WERE COMING THICK AND FAST...

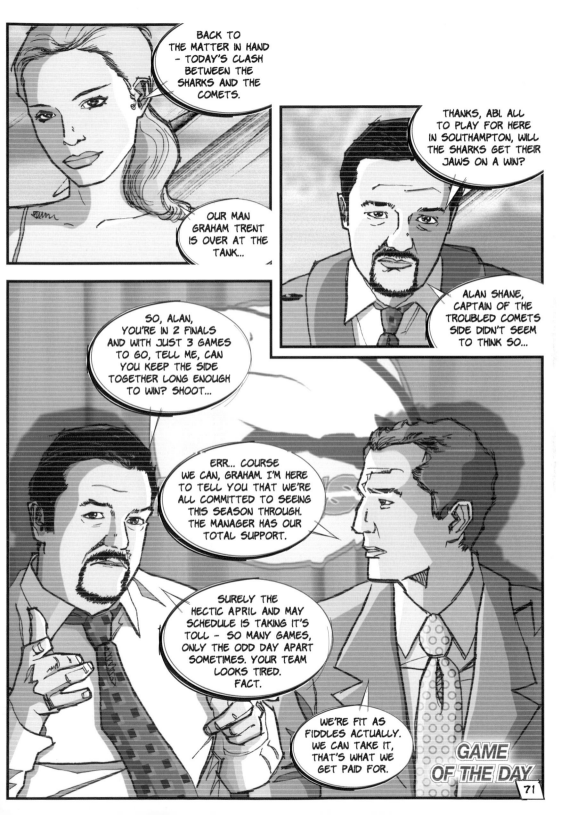

GAME
OF THE DAY

71

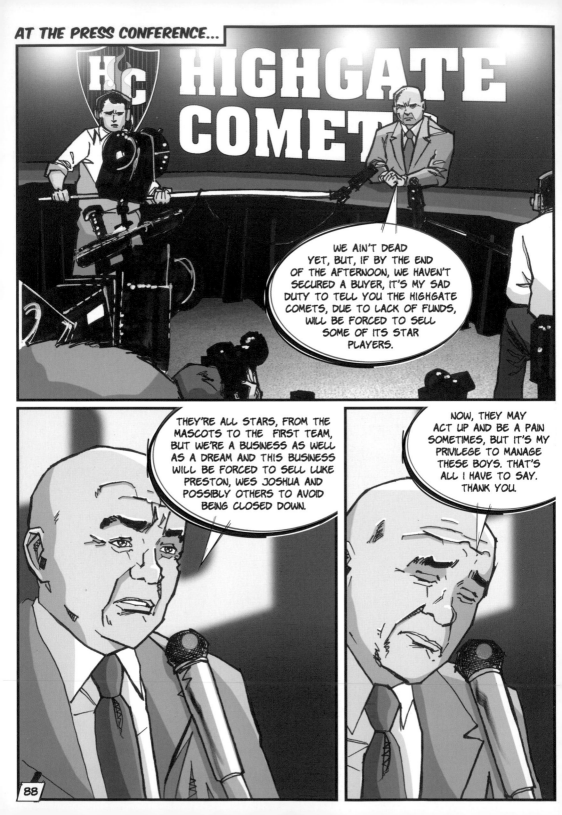

93

HOME TEAM

WHAT'S GOING ON?! AS IF I'M NOT UNDER ENOUGH PRESSURE!

LISTEN. WE'RE RED AND BLACK, THESE COLOURS BELONG TO THE HIGHGATE COMETS, US AND THE FANS. WE MAY HAVE BEEN THROUGH HELL, BUT IT STOPS NOW! WHATEVER THE FUTURE BRINGS, IF WE WIN OR LOSE WE DO IT *TOGETHER*.

HIGHGATE COMETS

HERE ARE THE TEAM SELECTIONS. NEITHER OF THEM HAVE COME HERE JUST TO PUT MEN BEHIND THE BALL.

21 DI FLORES
9 SHANE A (c)
11 CASSIDY
7 JOSHUA
8 SAMPILSON
10 PRESTON
17 FAKAMOTO
6 GOMO
5 DAVIS
2 MONK
13 TWINRIVERS

GAME OF THE DAY

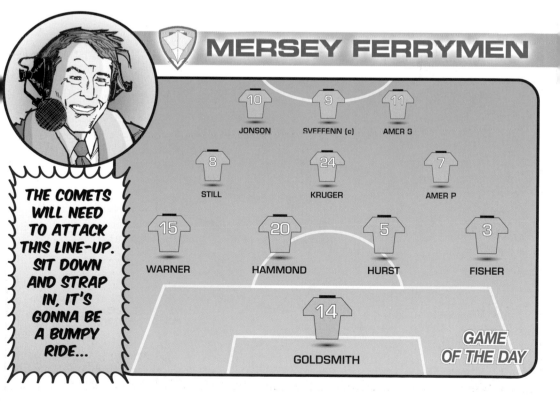

MERSEY FERRYMEN

THE COMETS WILL NEED TO ATTACK THIS LINE-UP. SIT DOWN AND STRAP IN, IT'S GONNA BE A BUMPY RIDE...

10 JONSON
9 SVEFFENN (c)
11 AMER S
8 STILL
24 KRUGER
7 AMER P
15 WARNER
20 HAMMOND
5 HURST
3 FISHER
14 GOLDSMITH

GAME OF THE DAY

43 MINUTES...
LUKE?
OK, IT'S PRESTON AND CASSIDY FLYING UP THE LEFT WING...
...WHICH IS QUITE POETIC REALLY AS, BARRING MIRACLES, THIS COULD WELL BE THE LAST COMETS GAME FOR LUKE PRESTON, WES JOSHUA AND POSSIBLY ZACK CASSIDY! LET'S SEE IF THEY CAN MAKE IT COUNT..!
DJ FAKAMOTO BACKING THEM UP. A LOVELY ONE-TWO THERE, CASSIDY... TO PRESTON... THIS IS MAGIC... STILL PRESTON! OH MY WORD!
ZACK?

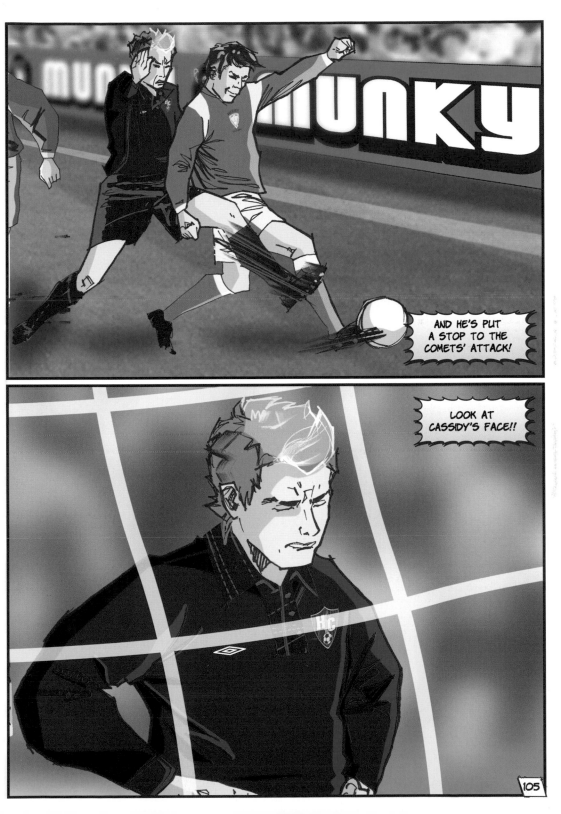

85 MINUTES...

AN UNREMARKABLE SECOND HALF ALTHOUGH THE FERRYMEN SEEM TO BE DOMINATING... SHANE...

SVEFFENN'S ON HIM... OH FOUL!

THAT'S GOT TO BE A RED CARD...

AND THE LAST KICK AS A COMET FOR SEVERAL PLAYERS...

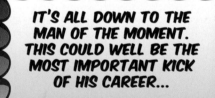

IT'S ALL DOWN TO THE MAN OF THE MOMENT. THIS COULD WELL BE THE MOST IMPORTANT KICK OF HIS CAREER...

TO BE CONTINUED...